*For Mum and Dad.*
W. S.

*For Marlene,*
*my little future archaeologist.*
A. S.

Text © 2021 Wenda Shurety
Illustrations © 2021 Andrea Stegmaier

First published in 2021
by Storyhouse Publishing
Malvern Villas, Bath BA1 5JS, UK
www.storyhousepublishing.com

ISBN 9781916281813

Designed by
Ali Halliday and Sue Mason

Printed in Heshan, Guangdong,
China by Leo Paper Products

# DIG!
# DIG!
# DIG!

## WENDA
## SHURETY

## ANDREA
## STEGMAIER

STORYHOUSE

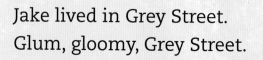

Jake lived in Grey Street.
Glum, gloomy, Grey Street.

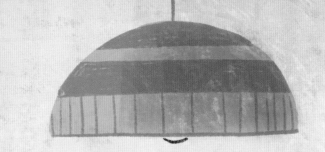

"Anywhere would be more exciting than here," he thought. He sighed and spun the globe on the window sill.

On the other side of
the world, he noticed a large island.

What would it be like to live there?
Did people walk
upside down?

Jake stared at the old vegetable patch through the window.

"I'm going to dig a hole to the other side of the world!"

He tore into the garden and started
to dig the soft earth with his hands.

Dig, **dig**, **dig.**

The hole grew to the size
of the kitchen sink.

The girl next door called through the fence.
"What are you doing?"

"I'm digging a hole to the other side
of the world," said Jake.

"I think you need a tool to dig. Will this help?"

Soon the girl was digging with Jake.

# Dig,
## dig,
### dig.

The hole grew to the size of a bath.

The boy next door peeped over the fence.

Jake looked up and said, "We're digging a hole to the
other side of the world. Would you like to come over?"

The boy appeared by the vegetable patch, driving a toy digger.
Jake smiled at him and the girl moved over to make room.

Soon the three of them
were digging away.

The hole grew to the size of a swimming pool

# Dig, dig, dig.

The girl over the road opened
the garden gate.
"What are you doing?"

"We're digging a hole to the other side of the world," said Jake.
"You won't get far with those tools. I'll get a trowel."

More children joined them.

Some took turns to loosen the earth,

while others scooped
it into piles.

Dig,

dig,

dig.

The hole grew . . .

and grew . . .

# until . . .

Big fat raindrops splattered on to the ground.
Everyone looked at each other.

"What should we do?" asked Jake.

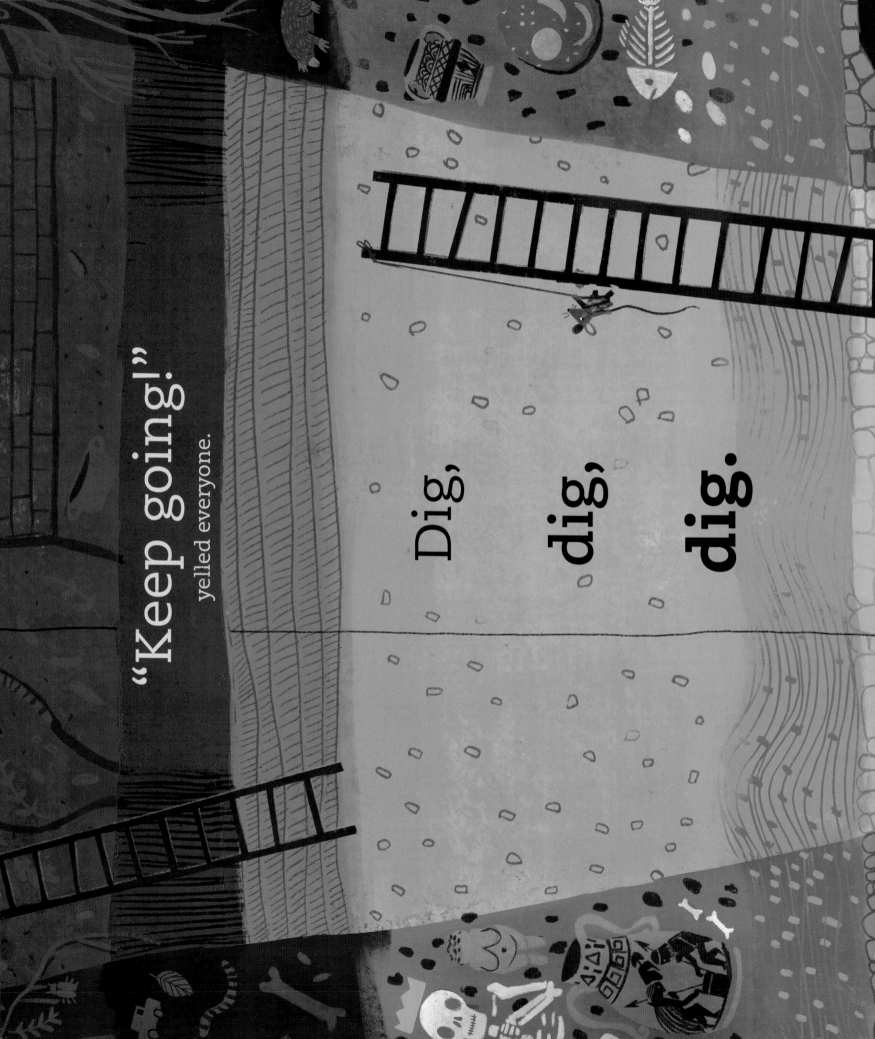

"Keep going!" yelled everyone.

Dig, dig, dig.

Dig, dig, dig!

"Look!" said the boy with the digger

Golden light appeared through
a gap in the bottom of the hole.

## "We've made it!"
squealed Jake with a
giant grin.

Everyone cheered!

Jake poked his head into the sunlight
at the other side of the world.

Did people *really* walk
uʍop ǝpᴉsdn . . . ?

You'll have to dig your own hole to find out!